THE MIDDLE-CHILD BLUES

Kristyn Crow

illustrated by David Catrow

G. P. Putnam's Sons • Penguin Young Readers Group

For Steven, with love. —K. C.

To Nancy, Mary Ellen, Sally, and Peggy—
from one of the ones in the middle. —D. C.

G. P. PUTNAM'S SONS
A division of Penguin Young Readers Group.
Published by The Penguin Group.
Penguin Group {USA} Inc., 375 Hudson Street, New York, NY 10014, U.S.A.
Penguin Group {Canada}, 90 Eglinton Avenue East, Suite 700, Toronto, Ontario M4P 2Y3, Canada
{a division of Pearson Penguin Canada Inc.}.
Penguin Books Ltd, 80 Strand, London WC2R 0RL, England.
Penguin Ireland, 25 St. Stephen's Green, Dublin 2, Ireland {a division of Penguin Books Ltd.}.
Penguin Group {Australia}, 250 Camberwell Road, Camberwell, Victoria 3124, Australia
{a division of Pearson Australia Group Pty Ltd}.
Penguin Books India Pvt Ltd, 11 Community Centre, Panchsheel Park, New Delhi - 110 017, India.
Penguin Group {NZ}, 67 Apollo Drive, Rosedale, North Shore 0632, New Zealand
{a division of Pearson New Zealand Ltd}.
Penguin Books {South Africa} {Pty} Ltd, 24 Sturdee Avenue, Rosebank, Johannesburg 2196, South Africa.
Penguin Books Ltd, Registered Offices: 80 Strand, London WC2R 0RL, England.

Manufactured in China by South China Printing Co. Ltd.
Design by Katrina Damkoehler. Text set in Instanter Bold.
The art was done in pencil and watercolor.

Library of Congress Cataloging-in-Publication Data
Crow, Kristyn.
The middle-child blues / Kristyn Crow ; illustrated by David Catrow.   p. cm.
Summary: A boy named Lee sings about all the miserable aspects of being a middle child.
{1. Stories in rhyme. 2. Middle-born children—Fiction. 3. Birth order—Fiction.
4. Brothers and sisters—Fiction. 5. Family life—Fiction. 6. Blues {Music}—Fiction.}
I. Catrow, David, ill. II. Title.
PZ8.3.C8858Mi 2009   {E}—dc22   2008030591

ISBN 978-0-399-24735-4
10 9 8 7 6 5 4 3 2 1

Well, first there was Raymond.

Uh-huh.

And then came Lee.

That's me.

Kate, she was next, so that made three.

Ray's the admired son.

Uh-huh.

Kate is the cute one.

Oh, yeah.

But me, I'm in-between. . . .

Hardly noticed.

Hardly seen.

I'm too big for Kate's playmates.
Ray's friends yell, "Beat it! Go!"

But when MY pals come over,
Kate and Raymond steal the show.

Why does Ray stay up later?
Shouldn't Kate have chores too?
My parents say, "HE'S older,
and SHE'S younger than you."

I've got the middle-child blues.
I feel forgotten and confused.
That's right, the middle-child blues.
And I am REALLY not amused.

I've got the

low-down

big-frown

sulkin'-all-around-town

bummed-out

MID-KID BLUES.

Ray can order a "Big Bun,"
and Kate's meal has a toy.
I get a plain cheeseburger
since I'm just the middle boy.

I can't ride with the babies,
or drive go-karts with Ray.
"You're too big!" "You're too little!"
That is ALL my parents say.

I'm not the shortest.
No way.
I'm not the tallest.
Oh, no.
I'm not the biggest and
I'm not the smallest.

I'm not the last.
No way.
I'm not the first.
Oh, no.
I'm not the best and
I'm not the worst.

I'm not the shiny engine
or the little red caboose.
I'm just a boring boxcar,
so I wonder, what's the use?

I've got the middle-child blues.
It is a curse I didn't choose.
That's right,
the middle-child blues.
Down to my
middle-sized shoes.

I've got the
low-down

big-frown

sulkin'-all-around-town
bummed-out

MID-KID BLUES.

So I'll get out my guitar.
I'll play the blues right here for you!

Look, I'm drawing a big crowd!
They say, "We're middle children too!"

And now there's four TV crews
and they put me on the news . . .
Singin' the
     MIDDLE-CHILD BLUES!

"I'm a kid like no other.
          Yeah, yeah.
Not just Ray and Kate's brother.
          No, no.
I'm Lee, and I'm blue.
Wish my folks had a clue.

Wooo wooo wooo woooo wooooooo."

Then Mom and Dad join the show.
"WE'RE middle children, you know."
"We just forgot for a while."
I pluck my guitar and smile.

We sing the middle-child blues.
And I am really quite amused!

We sing the

low-down

show-down

shakin'-up-the-
whole-town

big-time

MID-KID
BLUES!

Dad says, "Wow, that was great!
But it's getting rather late."
I take a bow right on beat.
The applause is pretty sweet.

And then I strut like a star,
to the middle of my car,

and do the middle-child snooze.

Oh, yeah.